espresso
education

Phonics

Kim's Big Bed

Diane Marwood

First published in 2011 by
Franklin Watts
338 Euston Road
London NW1 3BH

Franklin Watts Australia
Level 17/207 Kent Street
Sydney NSW 2000

Text and illustration © Franklin Watts 2011

The Espresso characters are originated and designed by Claire Underwood and Pesky Ltd.

The Espresso characters are the property of Espresso Education Ltd.

A CIP catalogue record for this book is available from the British Library.

ISBN: 978 1 4451 0422 5 (hbk)
ISBN: 978 1 4451 0435 5 (pbk)

Illustrations by Artful Doodlers Ltd.
Art Director: Jonathan Hair
Series Editor: Jackie Hamley
Series Designer: Matthew Lilly

Printed in China

Franklin Watts is a division of
Hachette Children's Books,
an Hachette UK company.

www.hachette.co.uk

Level 1 50 words
Concentrating on CVC words plus and, the, to

Level 2 70 words
Concentrating on double letter sounds and new letter sounds (ck, ff, ll, ss, j, v, w, x, y, z, zz) plus no, go, I

Level 3 100 words
Concentrating on new graphemes (qu, ch, sh, th, ng, ai, ee, igh, oa, oo, ar, or, ur, ow, oi, ear, air, ure, er) plus he, she, we, me, be, was, my, you, they, her, all

Level 4 150 words
Concentrating on adjacent consonants (CVCC/CCVC words) plus said, so, have, like, some, come, were, there, little, one, do, when, out, what

Kim got a big bed.

Kim put his ted and cat on the bed.

Kim put his dog and rat on the bed.

6

Kim got in the bed.

Kim got up!

red

log

Kim

hat

bed

14